Domino

Claire Masurel

illustrated by David Walker

Five puppies went out to play.
Four puppies were big.

One puppy was small.

HUMBOLDT PARK

Domino jumped!

But not as high as the big puppies.

Domino ran!

But not as fast as the big puppies.

Domino barked!

But not as loud as the big puppies.

A ball came bouncing by.

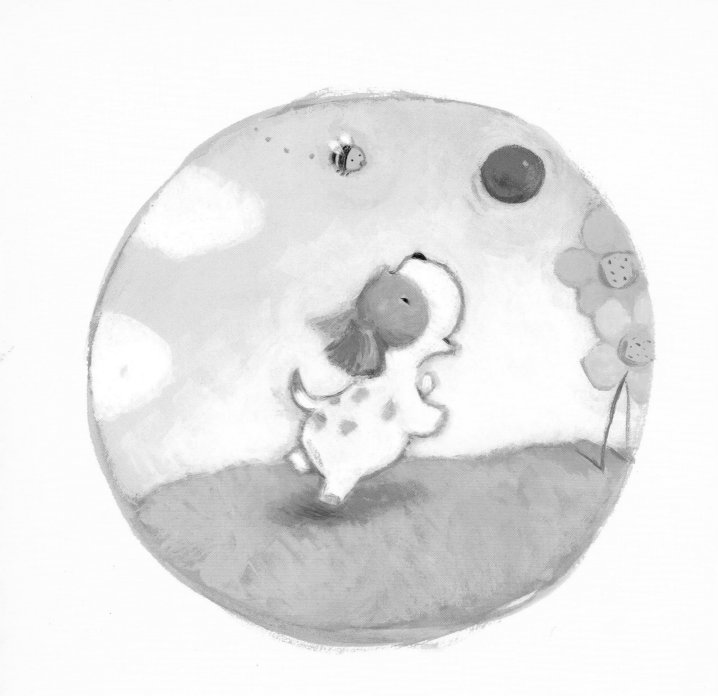

Domino jumped!

But he was too low.

Domino ran!
But he was too slow.

The ball rolled and rolled.

Four puppies barked!

Domino didn't bark.

He crawled under the fence.

He got the ball!